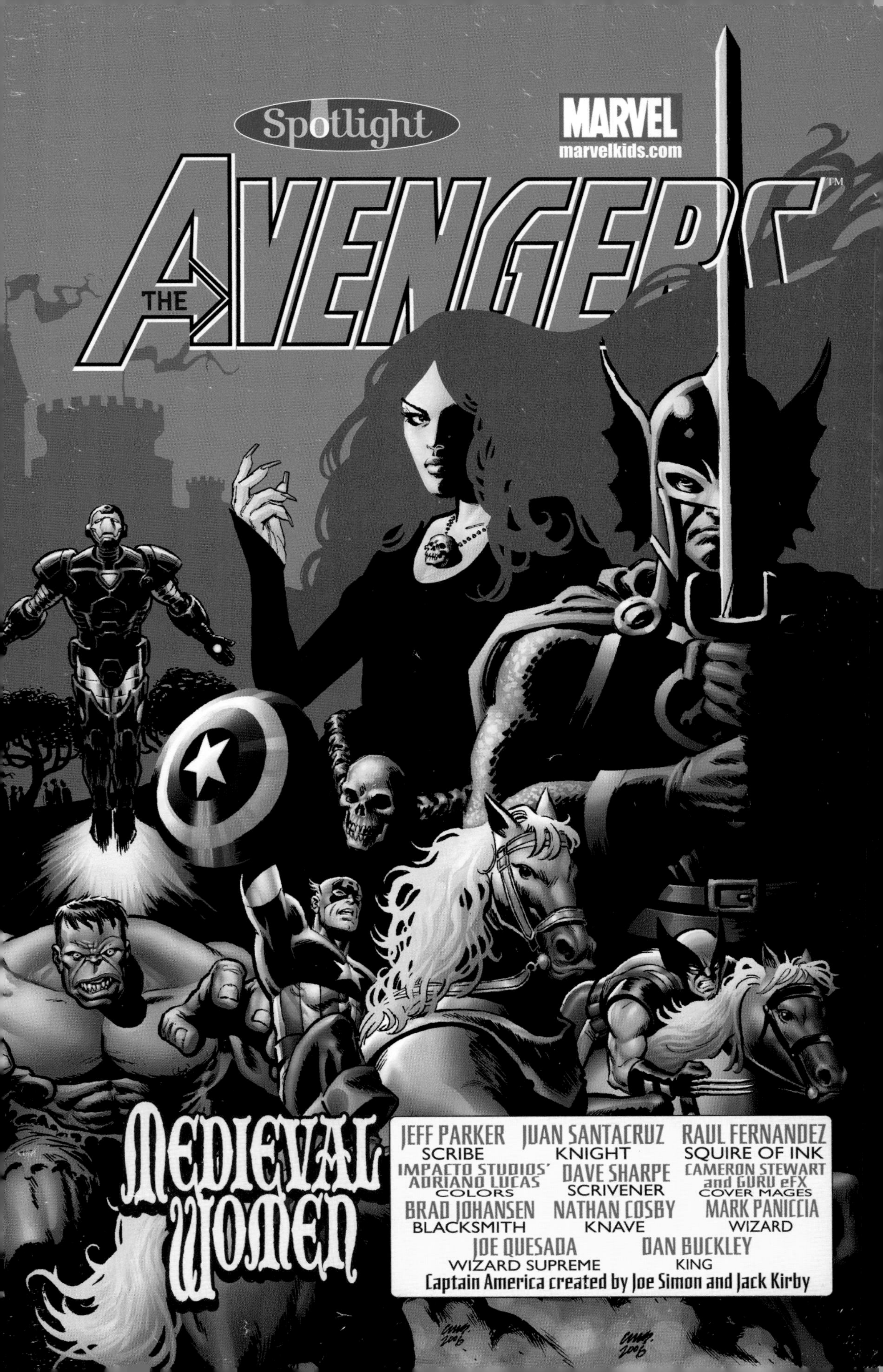
Spotlight
MARVEL
marvelkids.com
THE AVENGERS™
MEDIEVAL WOMEN
JEFF PARKER SCRIBE
JUAN SANTACRUZ KNIGHT
RAUL FERNANDEZ SQUIRE OF INK
IMPACTO STUDIOS' ADRIANO LUCAS COLORS
DAVE SHARPE SCRIVENER
CAMERON STEWART and GURU eFX COVER MAGES
BRAD JOHANSEN BLACKSMITH
NATHAN COSBY KNAVE
MARK PANICCIA WIZARD
JOE QUESADA WIZARD SUPREME
DAN BUCKLEY KING
Captain America created by Joe Simon and Jack Kirby

visit us at www.abdopublishing.com

Reinforced library bound edition published in 2013 by Spotlight, a division of the ABDO Group, 8000 West 78th Street, Edina, Minnesota 55439. Spotlight produces high-quality reinforced library bound editions for schools and libraries. Published by agreement with Marvel Entertainment, LLC. The stories, characters, and incidents mentioned are entirely fictional. All rights reserved. Used under authorization.

Printed in the United States of America, North Mankato, Minnesota.
052012
092012
♻ This book contains at least 10% recycled materials.

marvelkids.com

TM & © 2012 Marvel & Subs.

Library of Congress Cataloging-in-Publication Data

Parker, Jeff, 1966-

Medieval women / story by Jeff Parker ; art by Juan Santacruz. -- Reinforced library bound ed.

   p. cm. -- (Avengers)

"Marvel."

Summary: Includes bibliographical references and index.

ISBN 978-1-61479-016-7 (alk. paper)

1. Graphic novels. [1. Graphic novels.] I. Santacruz, Juan, ill. II. Title.

PZ7.7.P252Med 2012

741.5'973--dc23

2012000929

ISBN 978-1-61479-016-7 (reinforced library edition)

All Spotlight books are reinforced library binding and manufactured in the United States of America.

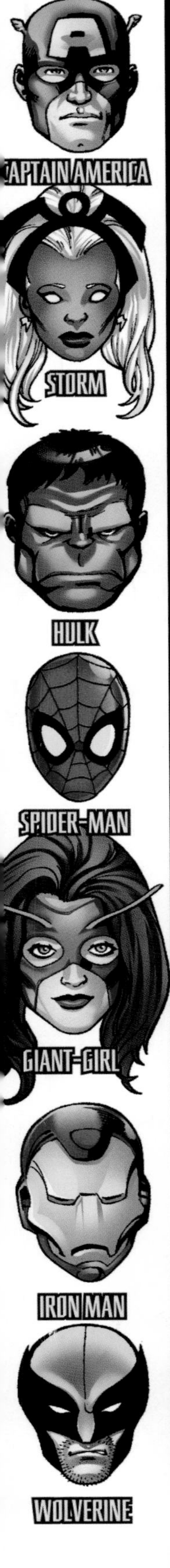
CAPTAIN AMERICA
STORM
HULK
SPIDER-MAN
GIANT-GIRL
IRON MAN
WOLVERINE

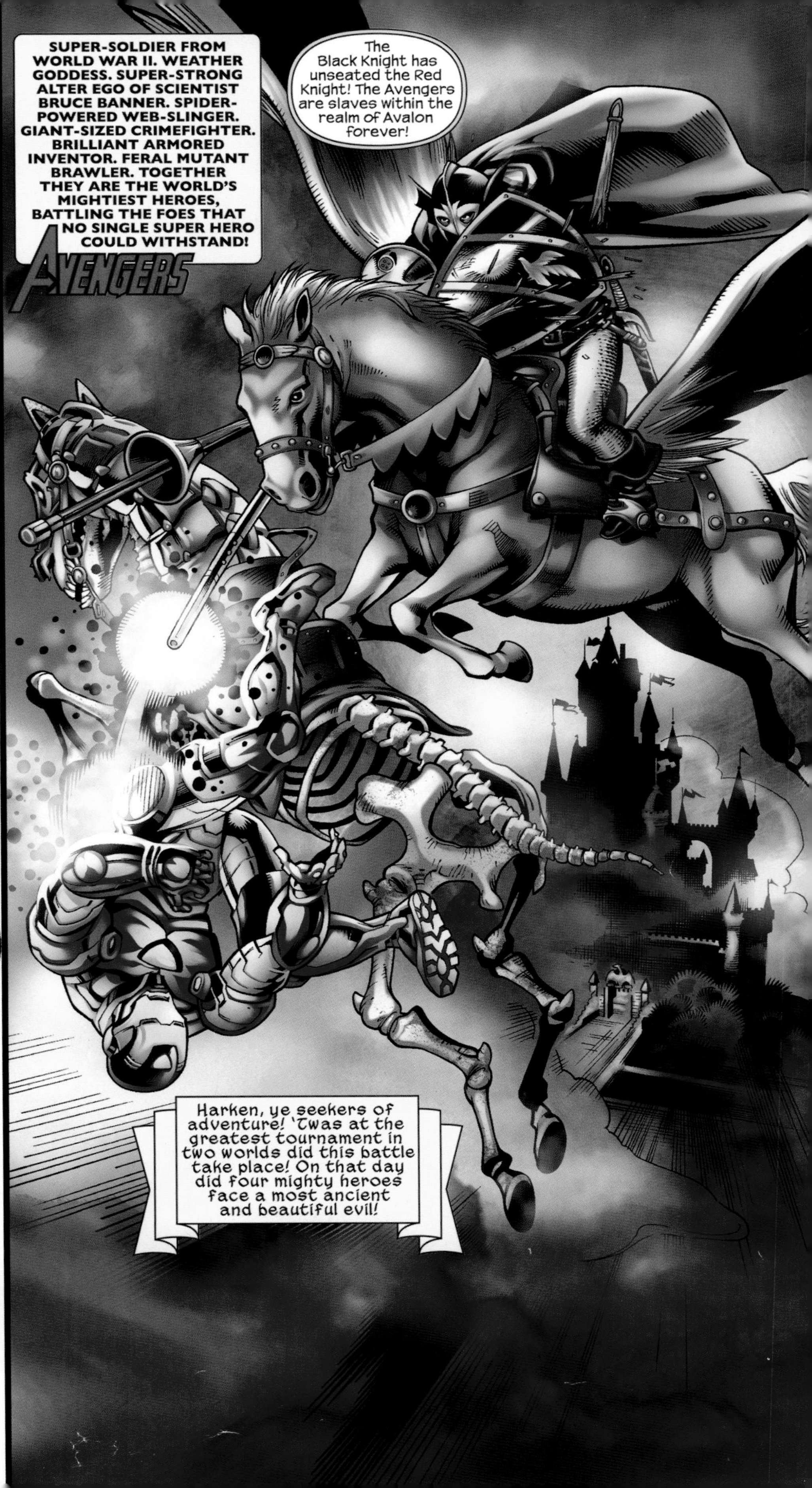
SUPER-SOLDIER FROM WORLD WAR II. WEATHER GODDESS. SUPER-STRONG ALTER EGO OF SCIENTIST BRUCE BANNER. SPIDER-POWERED WEB-SLINGER. GIANT-SIZED CRIMEFIGHTER. BRILLIANT ARMORED INVENTOR. FERAL MUTANT BRAWLER. TOGETHER THEY ARE THE WORLD'S MIGHTIEST HEROES, BATTLING THE FOES THAT NO SINGLE SUPER HERO COULD WITHSTAND!
AVENGERS
The Black Knight has unseated the Red Knight! The Avengers are slaves within the realm of Avalon forever!
Harken, ye seekers of adventure! 'Twas at the greatest tournament in two worlds did this battle take place! On that day did four mighty heroes face a most ancient and beautiful evil!

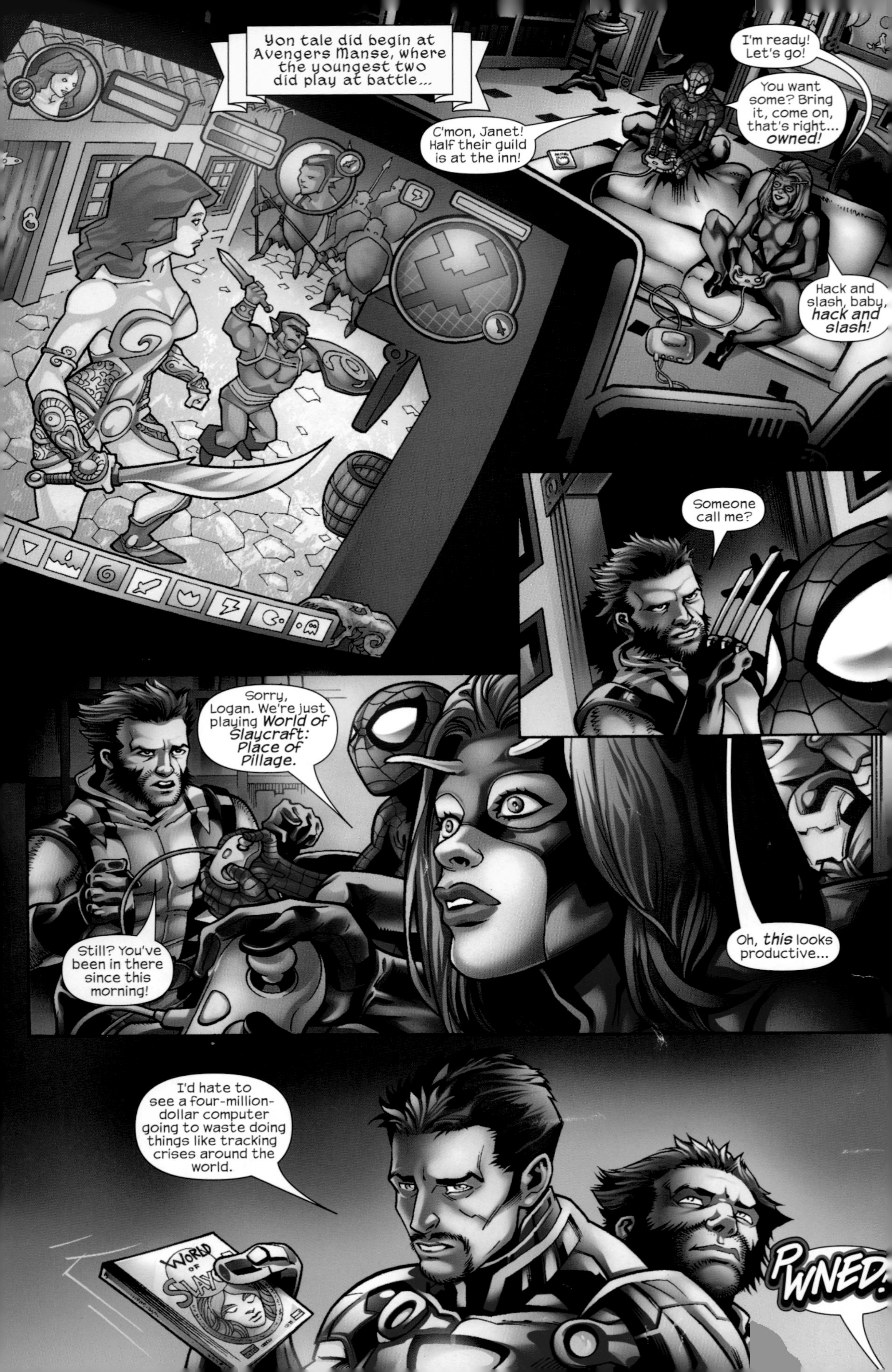

Yon tale did begin at Avengers Manse, where the youngest two did play at battle...
C'mon, Janet! Half their guild is at the inn!
I'm ready! Let's go!
You want some? Bring it, come on, that's right... *owned!*
Hack and slash, baby, *hack and slash!*
Someone call me?
Sorry, Logan. We're just playing *World of Slaycraft: Place of Pillage.*
Still? You've been in there since this morning!
Oh, *this* looks productive...
I'd hate to see a four-million-dollar computer going to waste doing things like tracking crises around the world.
PWNED!

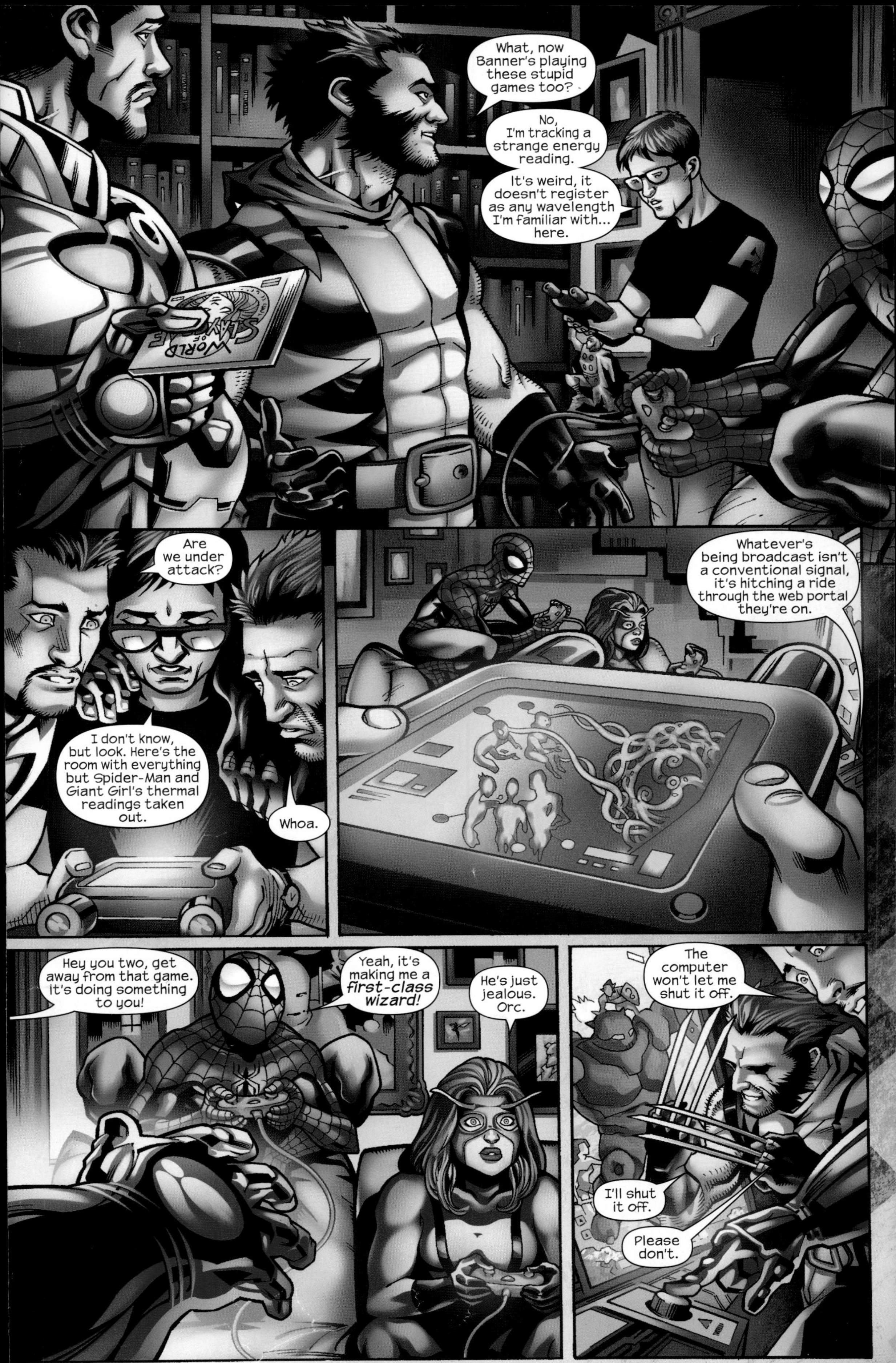
What, now Banner's playing these stupid games too?
No, I'm tracking a strange energy reading.
It's weird, it doesn't register as any wavelength I'm familiar with... here.
WORLD OF SLAYCRAFE
Are we under attack?
I don't know, but look. Here's the room with everything but Spider-Man and Giant Girl's thermal readings taken out.
Whoa.
Whatever's being broadcast isn't a conventional signal, it's hitching a ride through the web portal they're on.
Hey you two, get away from that game. It's doing something to you!
Yeah, it's making me a *first-class wizard!*
He's just jealous. Orc.
The computer won't let me shut it off.
I'll shut it off.
Please don't.

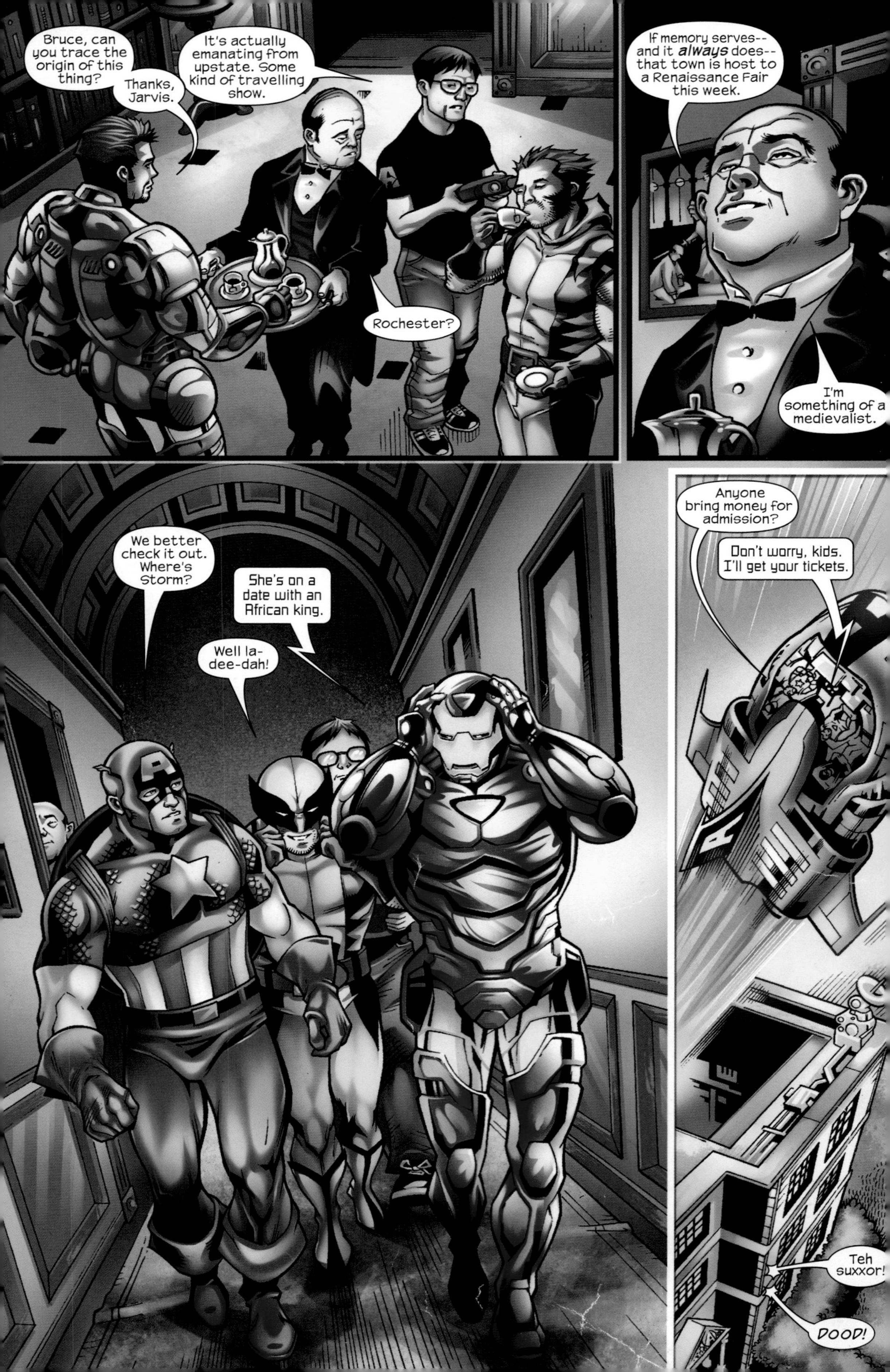

Bruce, can you trace the origin of this thing?
Thanks, Jarvis.
It's actually emanating from upstate. Some kind of travelling show.
Rochester?
If memory serves-- and it *always* does-- that town is host to a Renaissance Fair this week.
I'm something of a medievalist.
We better check it out. Where's Storm?
She's on a date with an African king.
Well la-dee-dah!
Anyone bring money for admission?
Don't worry, kids. I'll get your tickets.
Teh suxxor!
DOOD!

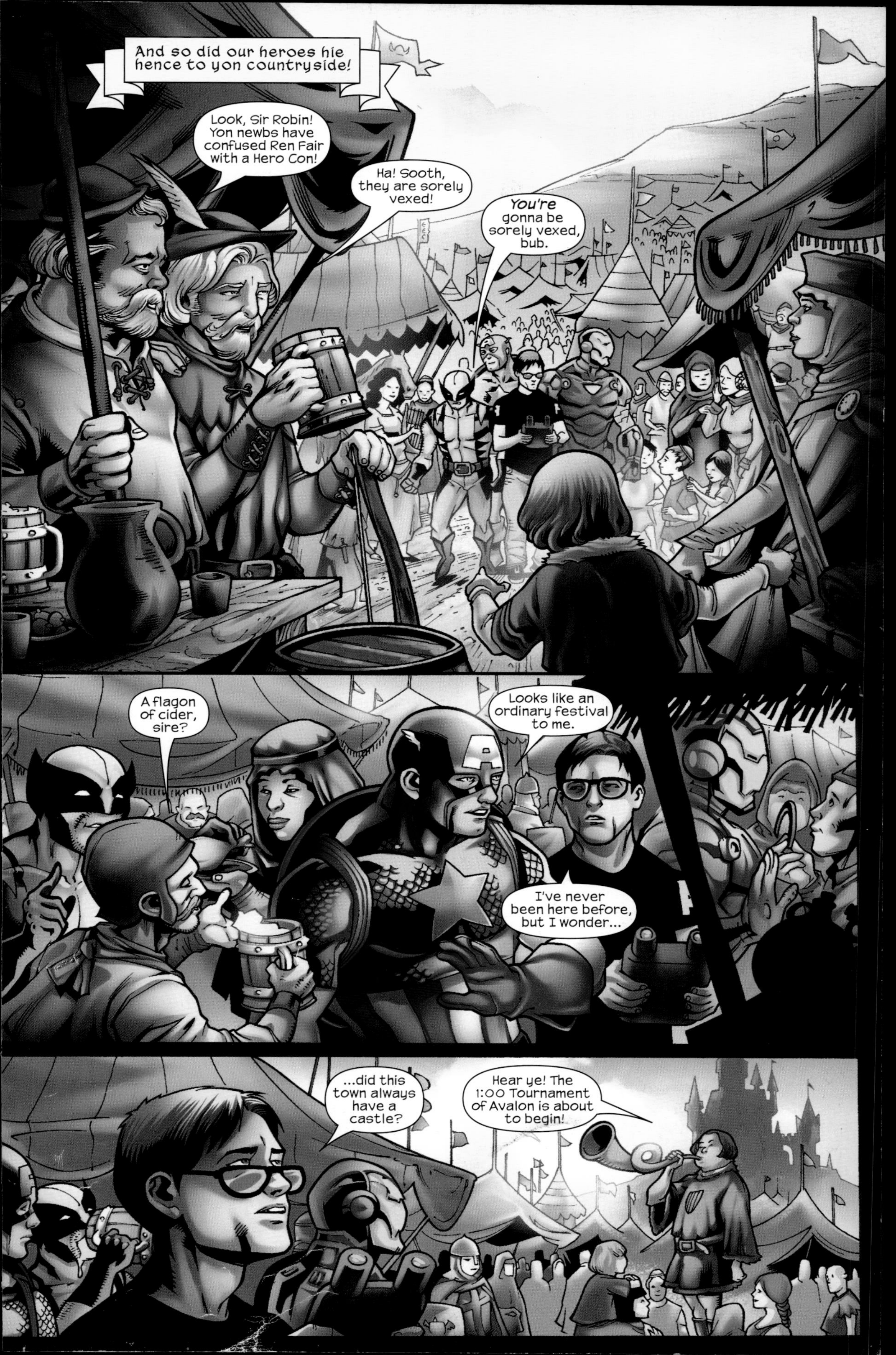
And so did our heroes hie hence to yon countryside!
Look, Sir Robin! Yon newbs have confused Ren Fair with a Hero Con!
Ha! Sooth, they are sorely vexed!
You're gonna be sorely vexed, bub.
A flagon of cider, sire?
Looks like an ordinary festival to me.
I've never been here before, but I wonder...
...did this town always have a castle?
Hear ye! The 1:00 Tournament of Avalon is about to begin!

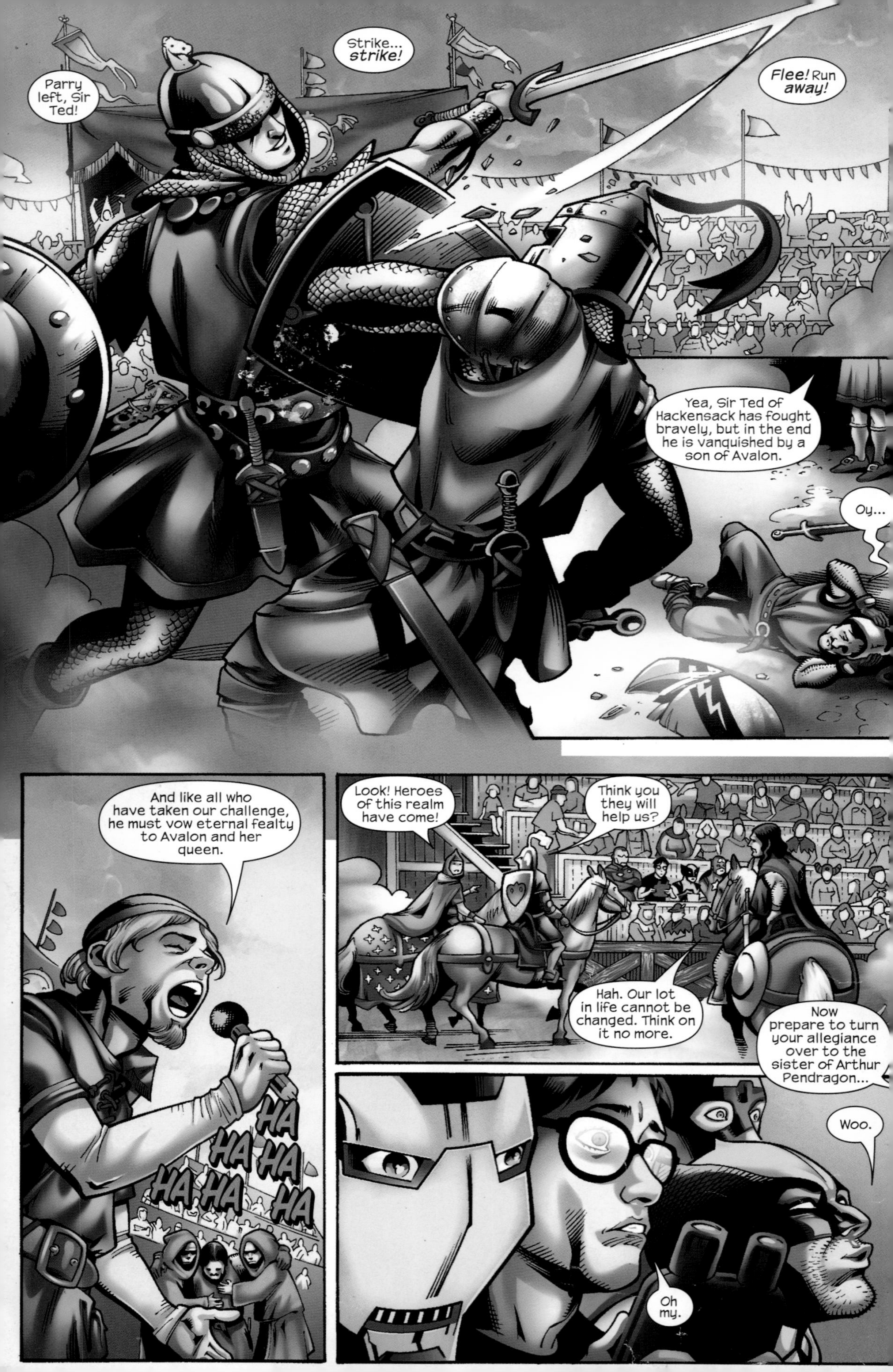
Parry left, Sir Ted!
Strike... strike!
Flee! Run away!
Yea, Sir Ted of Hackensack has fought bravely, but in the end he is vanquished by a son of Avalon.
Oy...
And like all who have taken our challenge, he must vow eternal fealty to Avalon and her queen.
HA HA HA HA HA HA
Look! Heroes of this realm have come!
Think you they will help us?
Hah. Our lot in life cannot be changed. Think on it no more.
Now prepare to turn your allegiance over to the sister of Arthur Pendragon...
Woo.
Oh my.

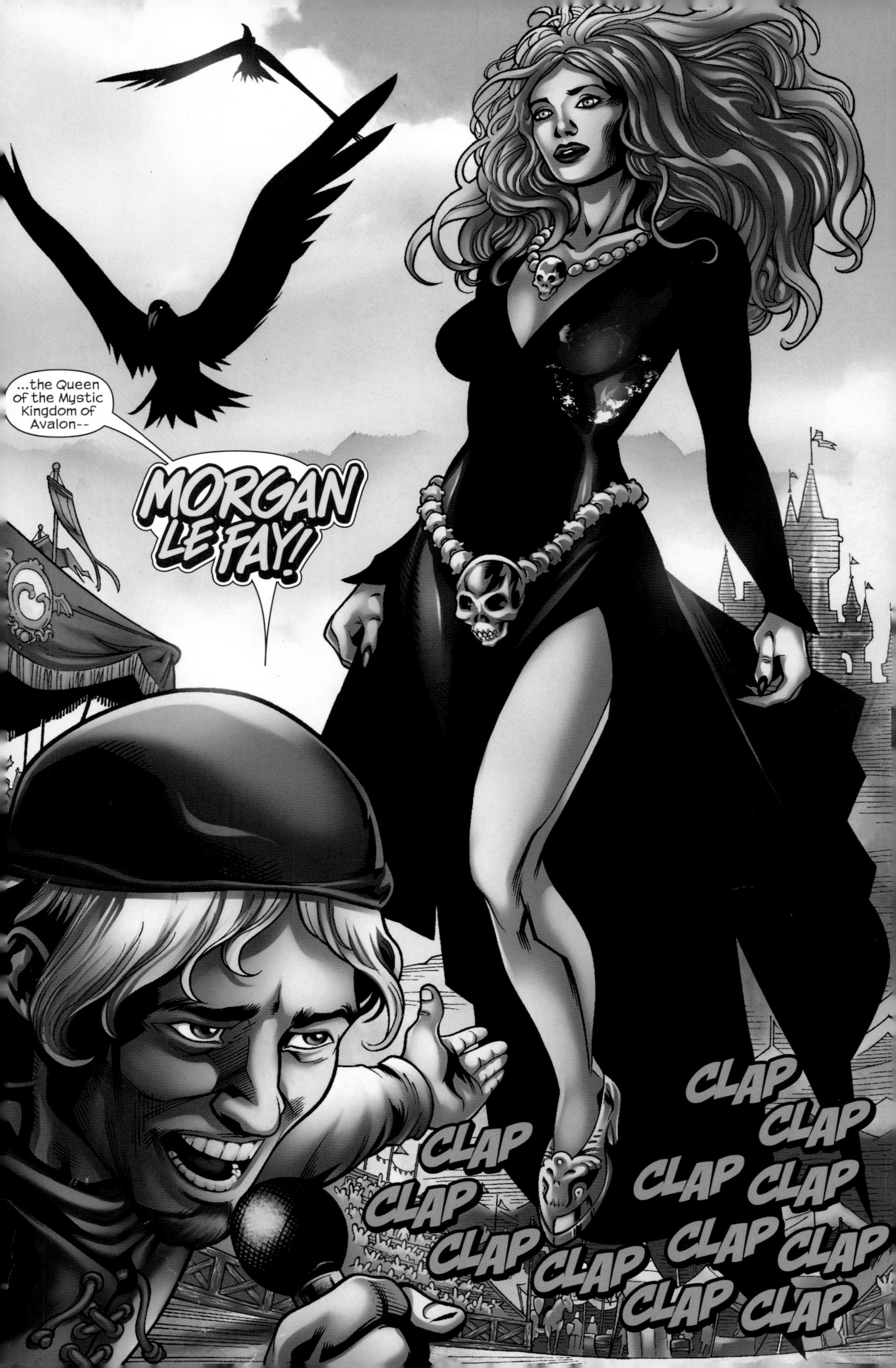
...the Queen of the Mystic Kingdom of Avalon--
MORGAN LE FAY!
CLAP CLAP CLAP CLAP CLAP CLAP CLAP CLAP CLAP CLAP CLAP CLAP CLAP

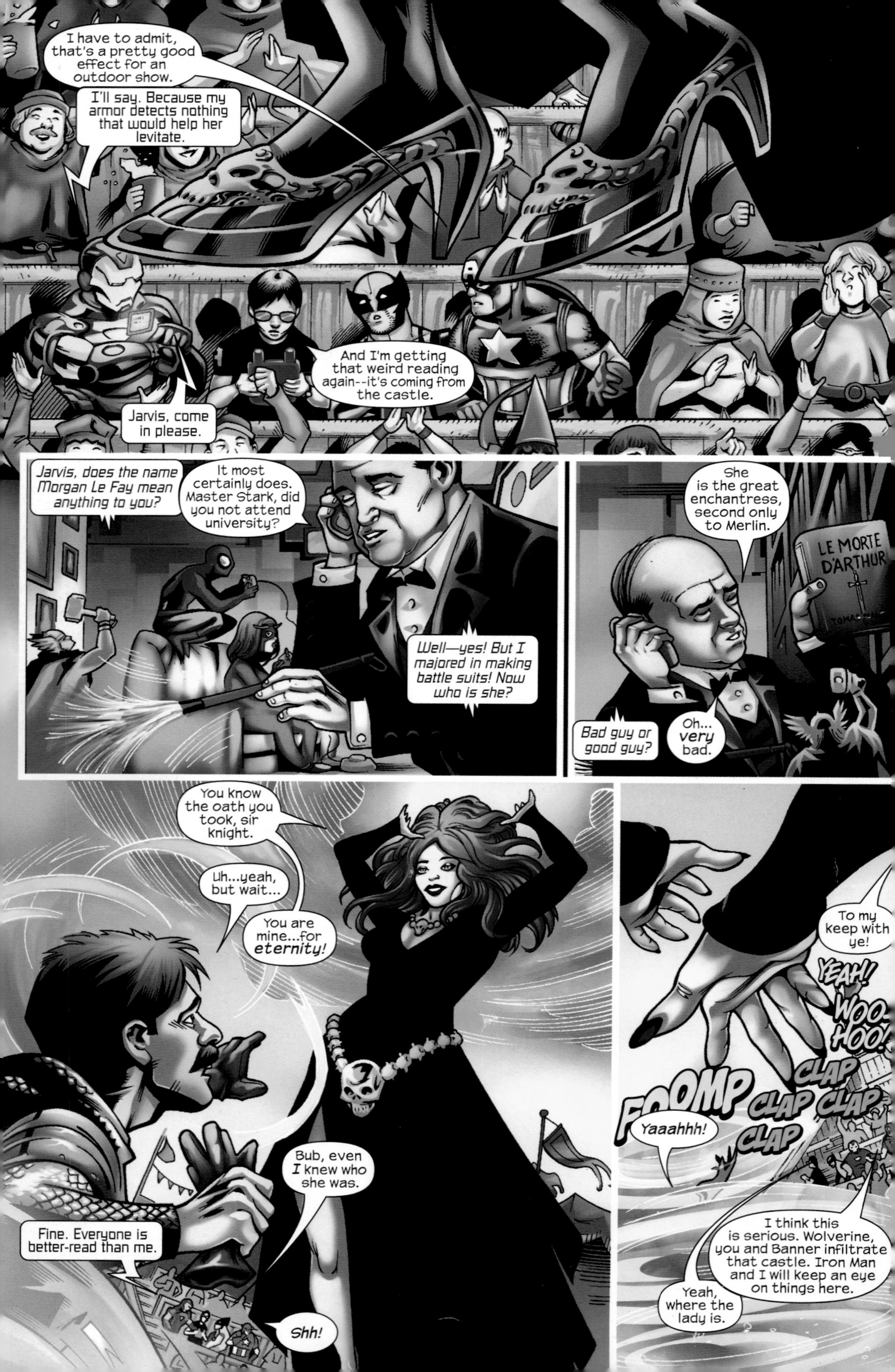

I have to admit, that's a pretty good effect for an outdoor show.
I'll say. Because my armor detects nothing that would help her levitate.
Jarvis, come in please.
And I'm getting that weird reading again--it's coming from the castle.
Jarvis, does the name Morgan Le Fay mean anything to you?
It most certainly does. Master Stark, did you not attend university?
Well—yes! But I majored in making battle suits! Now who is she?
She is the great enchantress, second only to Merlin.
LE MORTE D'ARTHUR
Bad guy or good guy?
Oh... very bad.
You know the oath you took, sir knight.
Uh...yeah, but wait...
You are mine...for eternity!
Bub, even I knew who she was.
Fine. Everyone is better-read than me.
Shh!
To my keep with ye!
YEAH!
WOO-HOO!
FOOMP
CLAP CLAP CLAP CLAP
Yaaahhh!
I think this is serious. Wolverine, you and Banner infiltrate that castle. Iron Man and I will keep an eye on things here.
Yeah, where the lady is.

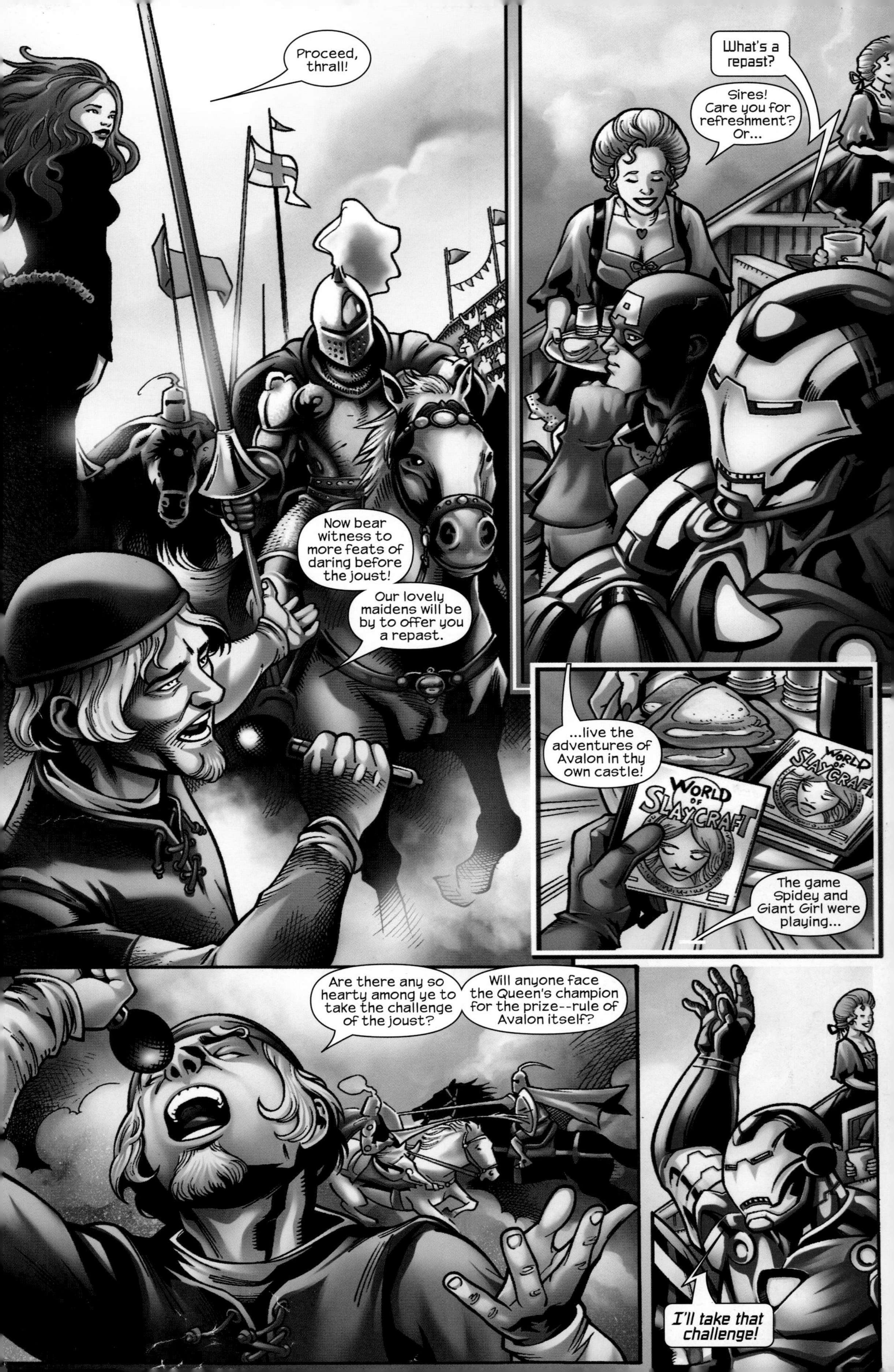
Proceed, thrall!
What's a repast?
Sires! Care you for refreshment? Or...
Now bear witness to more feats of daring before the joust!
Our lovely maidens will be by to offer you a repast.
...live the adventures of Avalon in thy own castle!
WORLD OF SLAYCRAFT
WORLD OF SLAYCRAFT
The game Spidey and Giant Girl were playing...
Are there any so hearty among ye to take the challenge of the joust?
Will anyone face the Queen's champion for the prize--rule of Avalon itself?
I'll take that challenge!

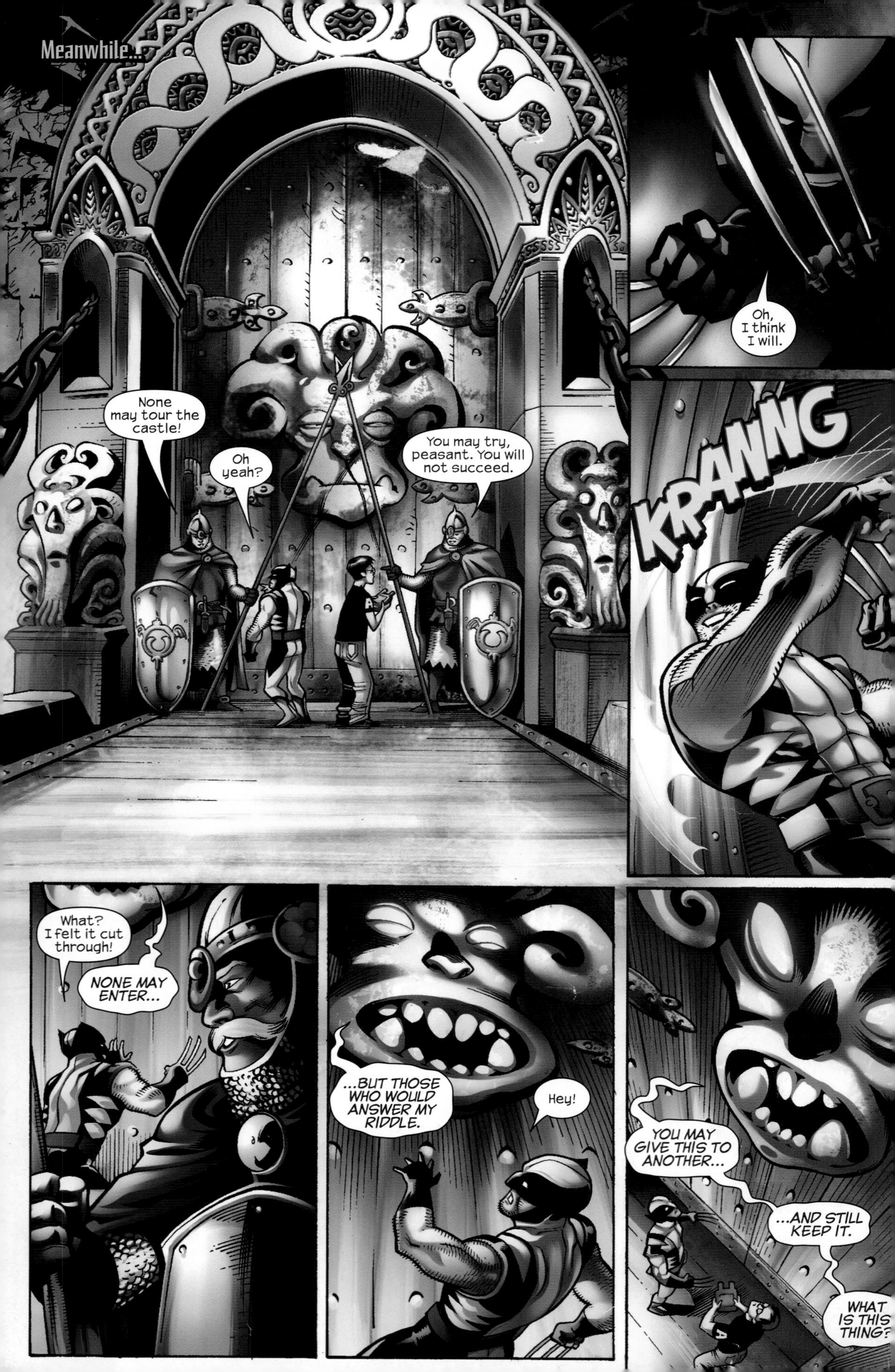
Meanwhile...
None may tour the castle!
Oh yeah?
You may try, peasant. You will not succeed.
Oh, I think I will.
KRANNG
What? I felt it cut through!
NONE MAY ENTER...
...BUT THOSE WHO WOULD ANSWER MY RIDDLE.
Hey!
YOU MAY GIVE THIS TO ANOTHER...
...AND STILL KEEP IT.
WHAT IS THIS THING?

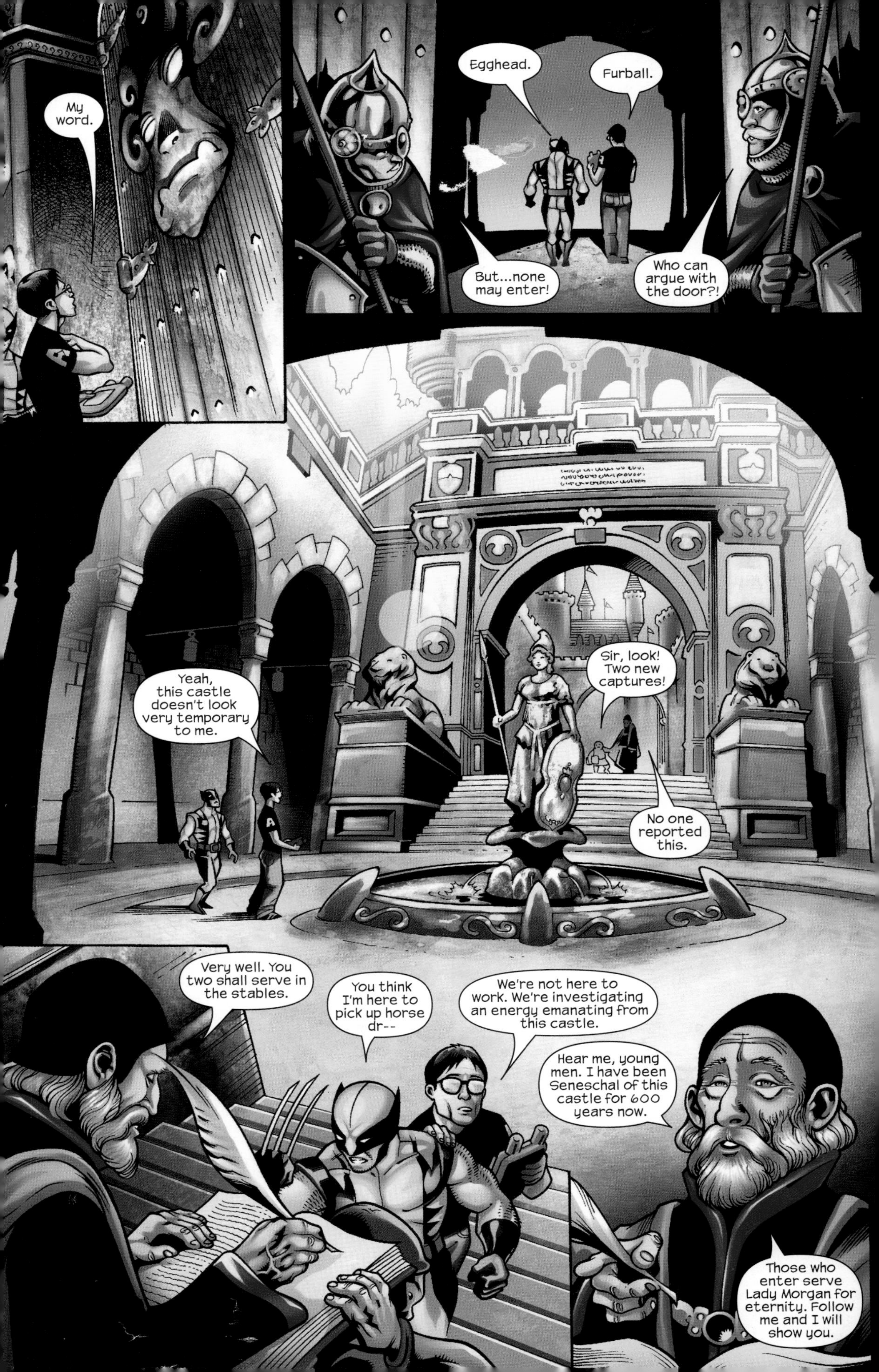
My word.
Egghead.
Furball.
But...none may enter!
Who can argue with the door?!
Yeah, this castle doesn't look very temporary to me.
Sir, look! Two new captures!
No one reported this.
Very well. You two shall serve in the stables.
You think I'm here to pick up horse dr--
We're not here to work. We're investigating an energy emanating from this castle.
Hear me, young men. I have been Seneschal of this castle for 600 years now.
Those who enter serve Lady Morgan for eternity. Follow me and I will show you.

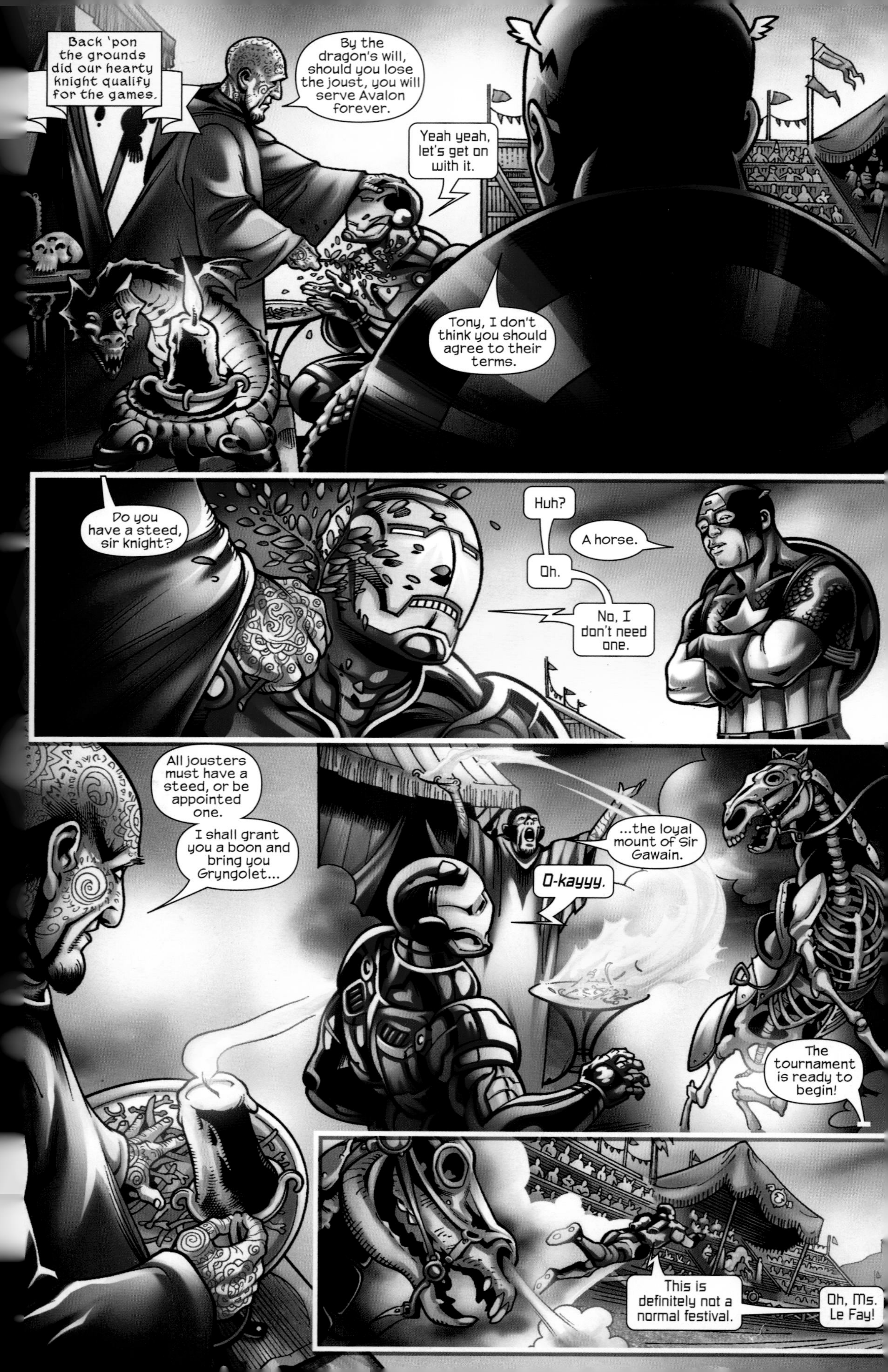

Back 'pon the grounds did our hearty knight qualify for the games.
By the dragon's will, should you lose the joust, you will serve Avalon forever.
Yeah yeah, let's get on with it.
Tony, I don't think you should agree to their terms.
Do you have a steed, sir knight?
Huh?
A horse.
Oh.
No, I don't need one.
All jousters must have a steed, or be appointed one.
I shall grant you a boon and bring you Gryngolet...
...the loyal mount of Sir Gawain.
O-kayyy.
The tournament is ready to begin!
This is definitely not a normal festival.
Oh, Ms. Le Fay!

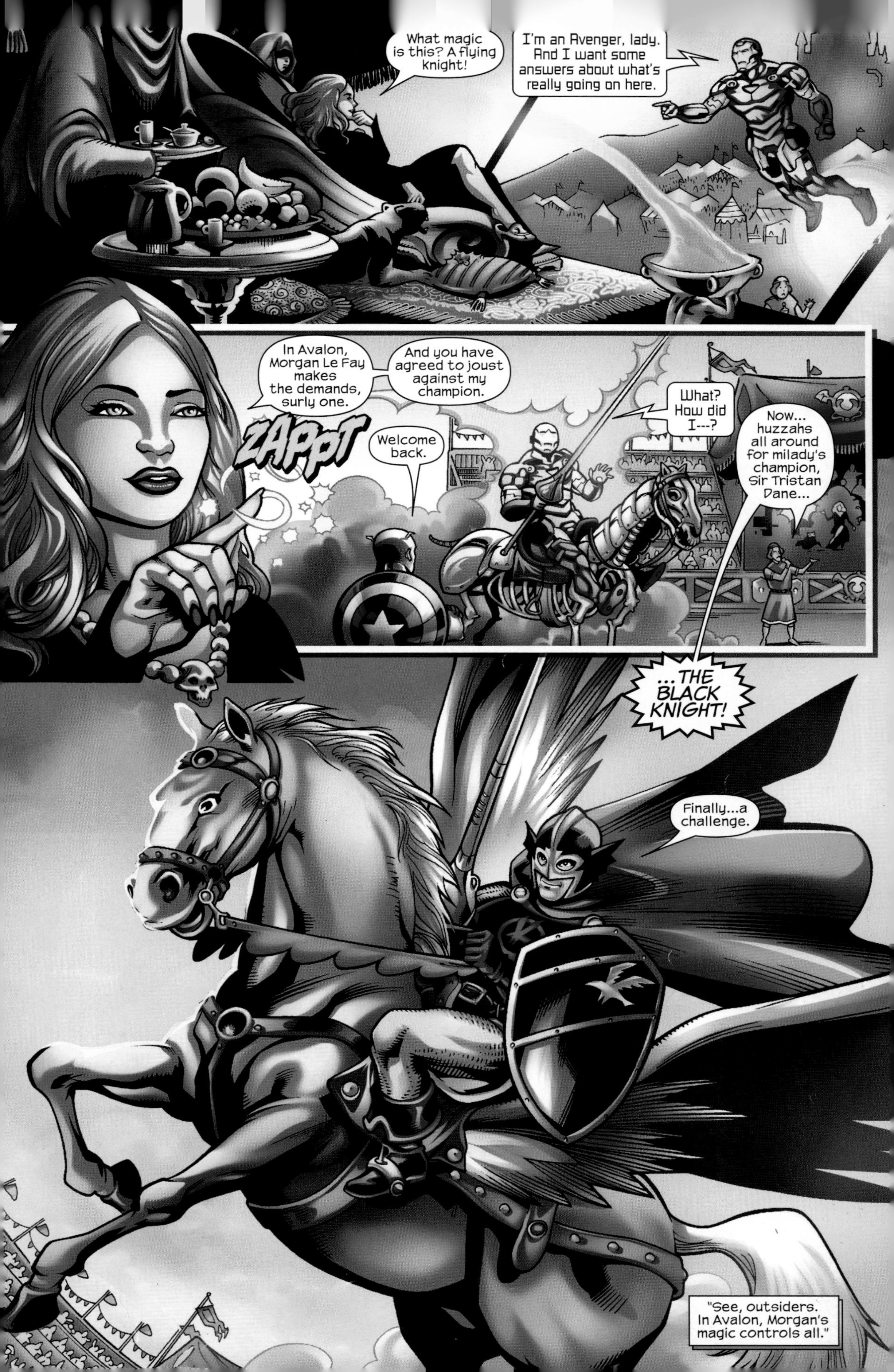
What magic is this? A flying knight!
I'm an Avenger, lady. And I want some answers about what's really going on here.
In Avalon, Morgan Le Fay makes the demands, surly one.
And you have agreed to joust against my champion.
ZAPPT
Welcome back.
What? How did I---?
Now... huzzahs all around for milady's champion, Sir Tristan Dane...
...THE BLACK KNIGHT!
Finally...a challenge.
"See, outsiders. In Avalon, Morgan's magic controls all."

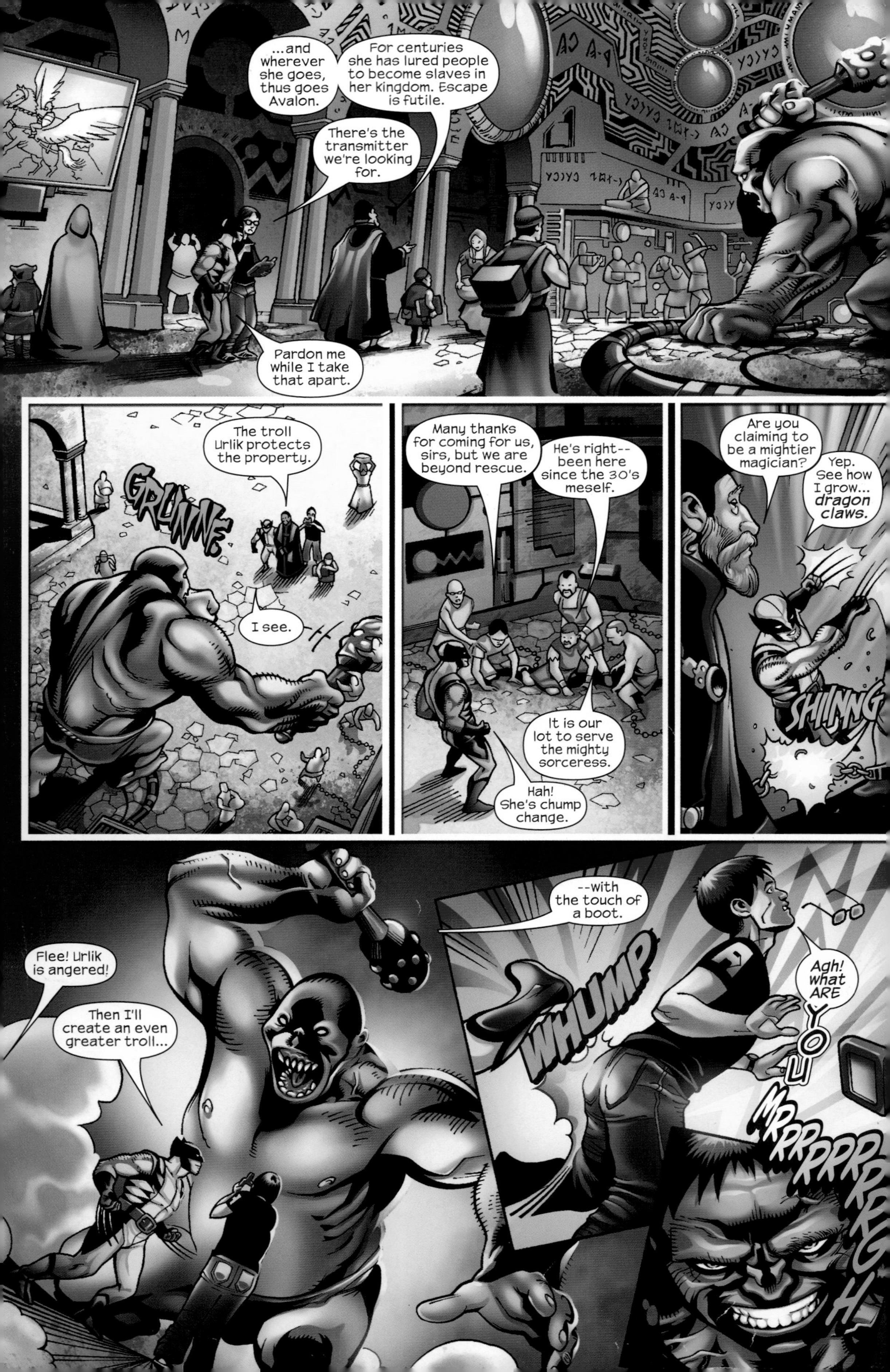
...and wherever she goes, thus goes Avalon.
For centuries she has lured people to become slaves in her kingdom. Escape is futile.
There's the transmitter we're looking for.
Pardon me while I take that apart.
The troll Urlik protects the property.
GRUNNE
I see.
Many thanks for coming for us, sirs, but we are beyond rescue.
He's right--been here since the 30's meself.
It is our lot to serve the mighty sorceress.
Hah! She's chump change.
Are you claiming to be a mightier magician?
Yep. See how I grow... dragon claws.
SHIINNG
Flee! Urlik is angered!
Then I'll create an even greater troll...
--with the touch of a boot.
WHUMP
Agh! What ARE YOU
MRRRRRRRRRGH

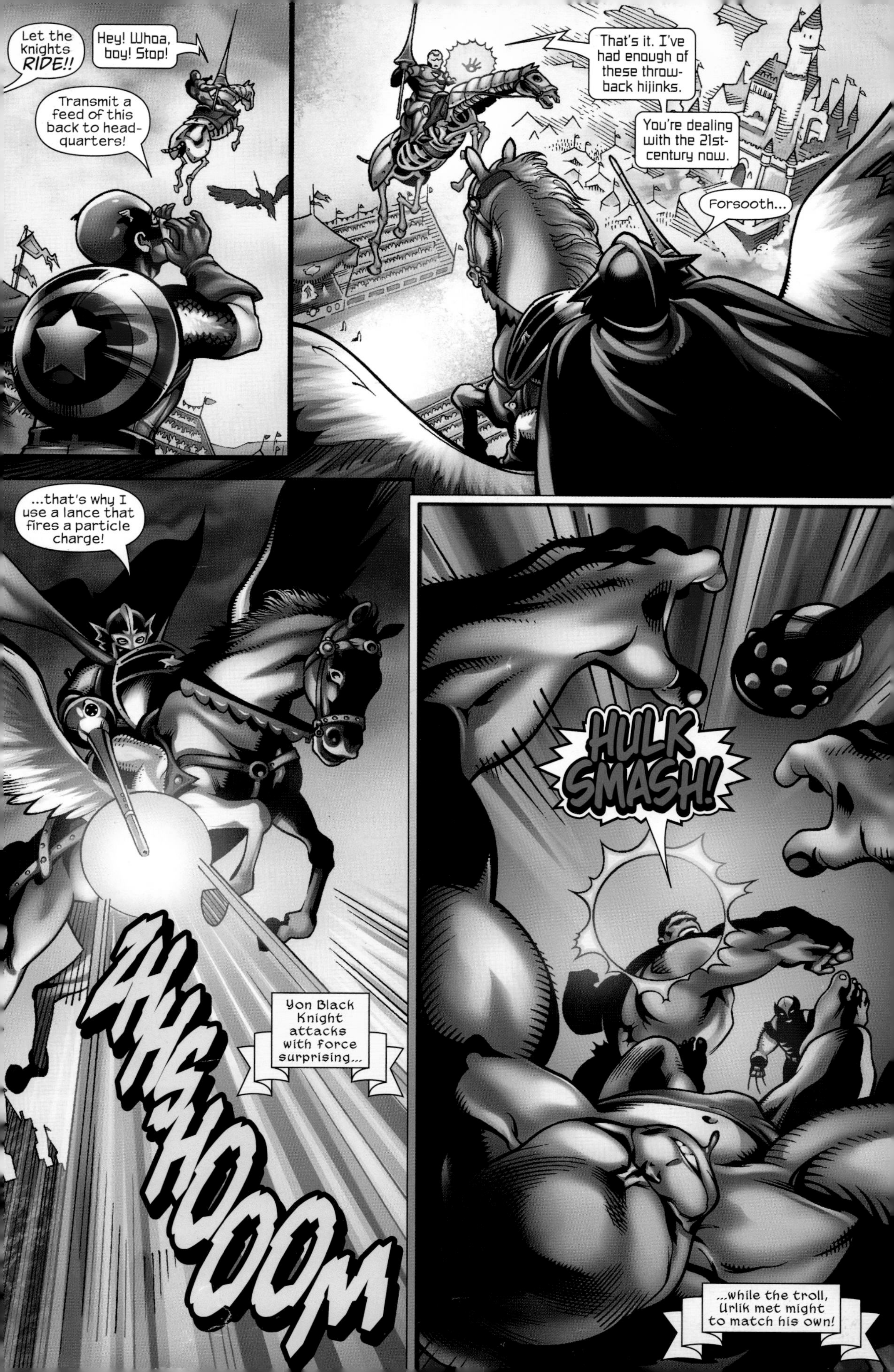
Let the knights RIDE!!
Hey! Whoa, boy! Stop!
Transmit a feed of this back to head-quarters!
That's it. I've had enough of these throw-back hijinks.
You're dealing with the 21st-century now.
Forsooth...
...that's why I use a lance that fires a particle charge!
ZHSHOOOM
Yon Black Knight attacks with force surprising...
HULK SMASH!
...while the troll, Urlik met might to match his own!

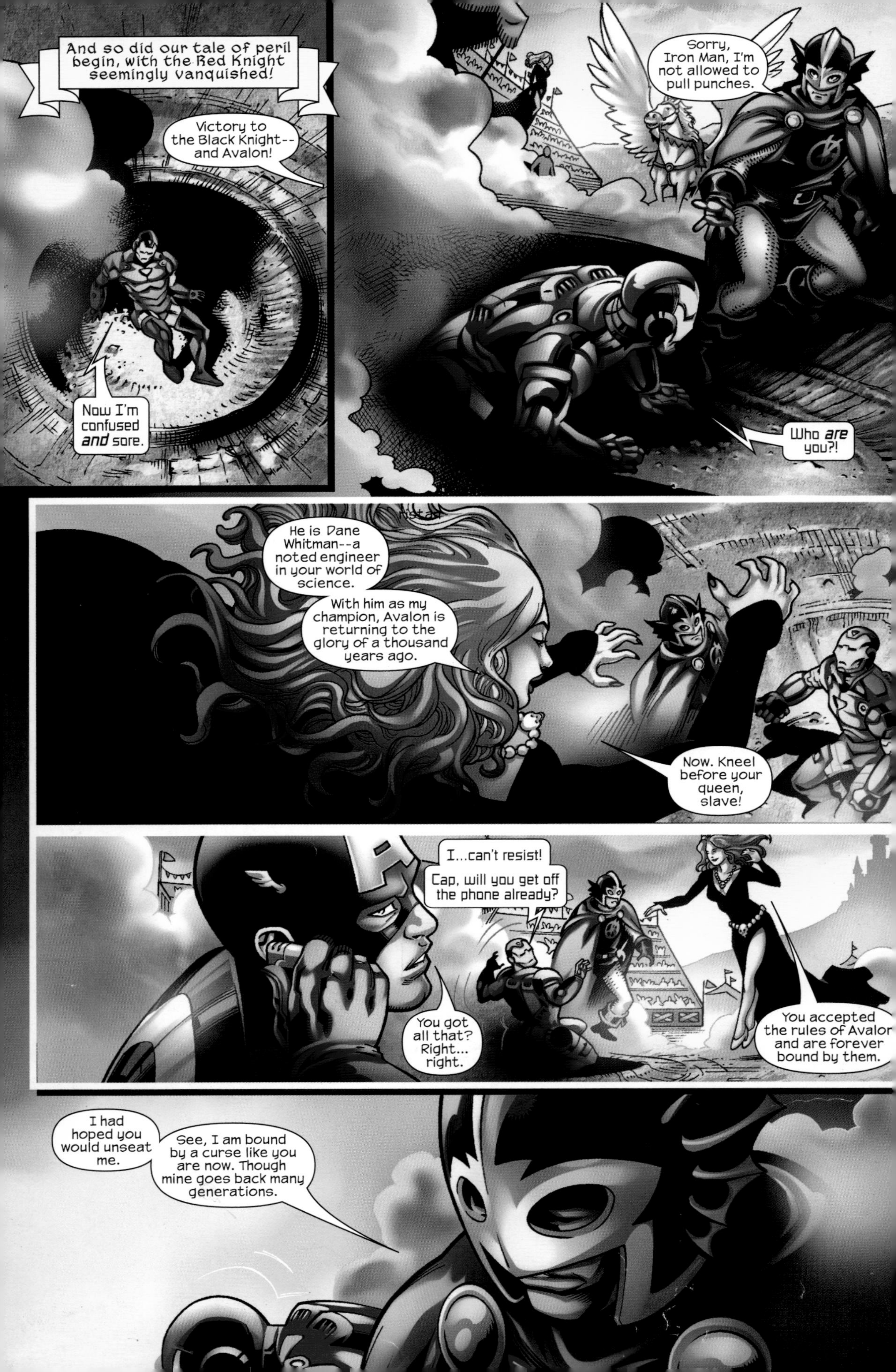
And so did our tale of peril begin, with the Red Knight seemingly vanquished!
Victory to the Black Knight-- and Avalon!
Now I'm confused *and* sore.
Sorry, Iron Man, I'm not allowed to pull punches.
Who *are* you?!
He is Dane Whitman--a noted engineer in your world of science.
With him as my champion, Avalon is returning to the glory of a thousand years ago.
Now. Kneel before your queen, slave!
I...can't resist!
Cap, will you get off the phone already?
You got all that? Right... right.
You accepted the rules of Avalon and are forever bound by them.
I had hoped you would unseat me.
See, I am bound by a curse like you are now. Though mine goes back many generations.

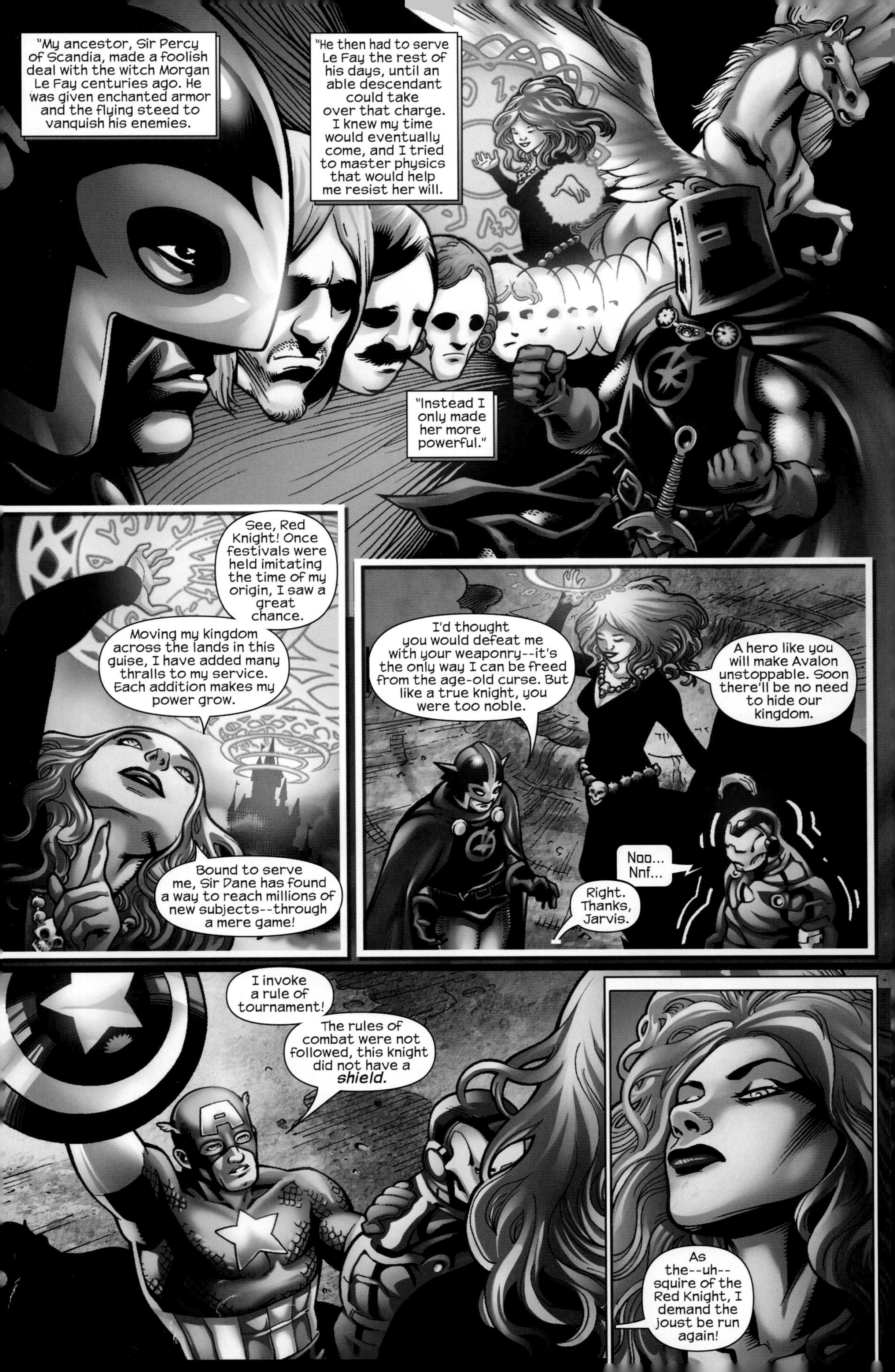
"My ancestor, Sir Percy of Scandia, made a foolish deal with the witch Morgan Le Fay centuries ago. He was given enchanted armor and the flying steed to vanquish his enemies.
"He then had to serve Le Fay the rest of his days, until an able descendant could take over that charge. I knew my time would eventually come, and I tried to master physics that would help me resist her will.
"Instead I only made her more powerful."
See, Red Knight! Once festivals were held imitating the time of my origin, I saw a great chance.
Moving my kingdom across the lands in this guise, I have added many thralls to my service. Each addition makes my power grow.
Bound to serve me, Sir Dane has found a way to reach millions of new subjects--through a mere game!
I'd thought you would defeat me with your weaponry--it's the only way I can be freed from the age-old curse. But like a true knight, you were too noble.
A hero like you will make Avalon unstoppable. Soon there'll be no need to hide our kingdom.
Noo... Nnf...
Right. Thanks, Jarvis.
I invoke a rule of tournament!
The rules of combat were not followed, this knight did not have a *shield.*
As the--uh--squire of the Red Knight, I demand the joust be run again!

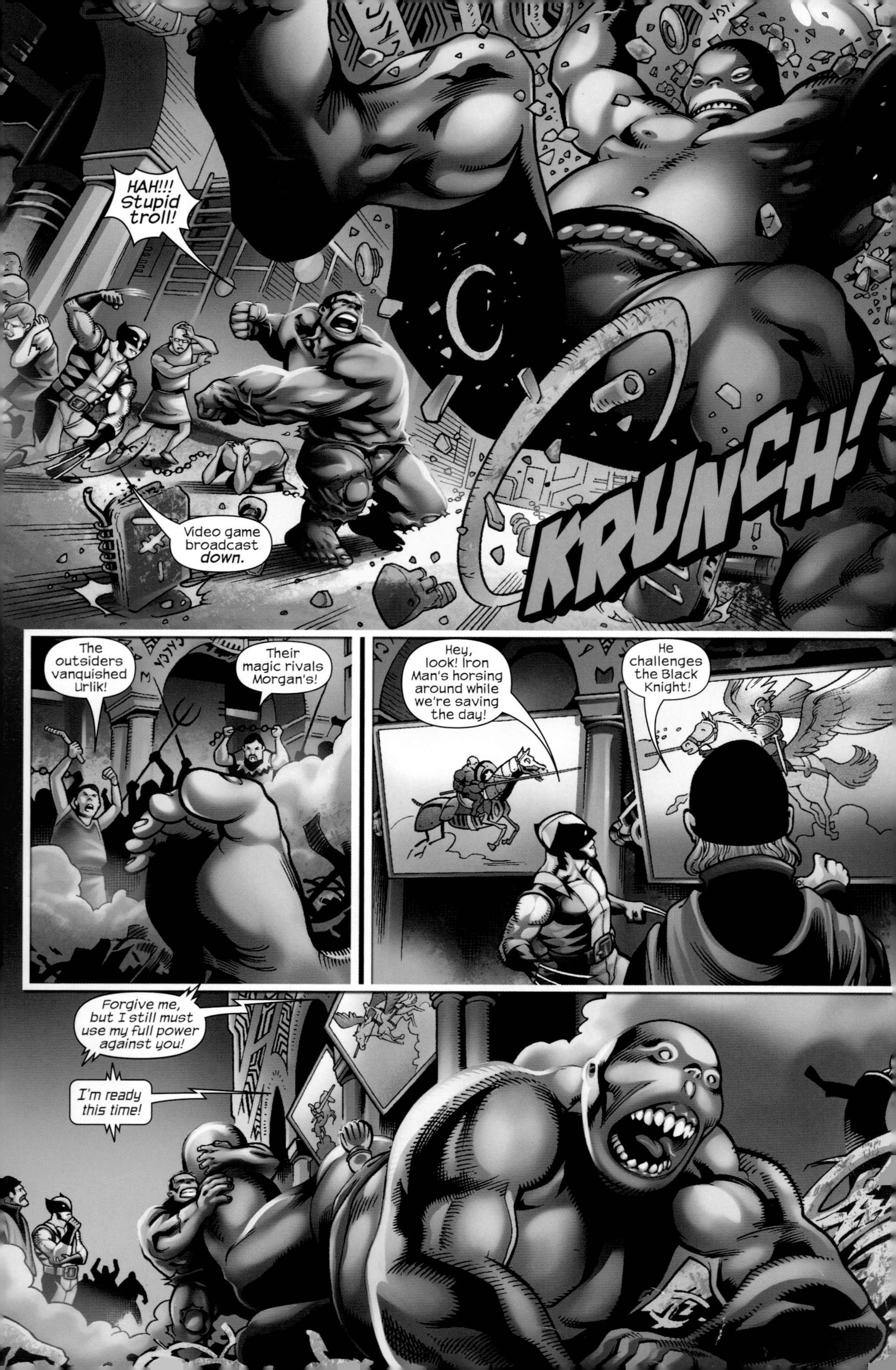
HAH!!! Stupid troll!
Video game broadcast down.
KRUNCH!
The outsiders vanquished Urlik!
Their magic rivals Morgan's!
Hey, look! Iron Man's horsing around while we're saving the day!
He challenges the Black Knight!
Forgive me, but I still must use my full power against you!
I'm ready this time!

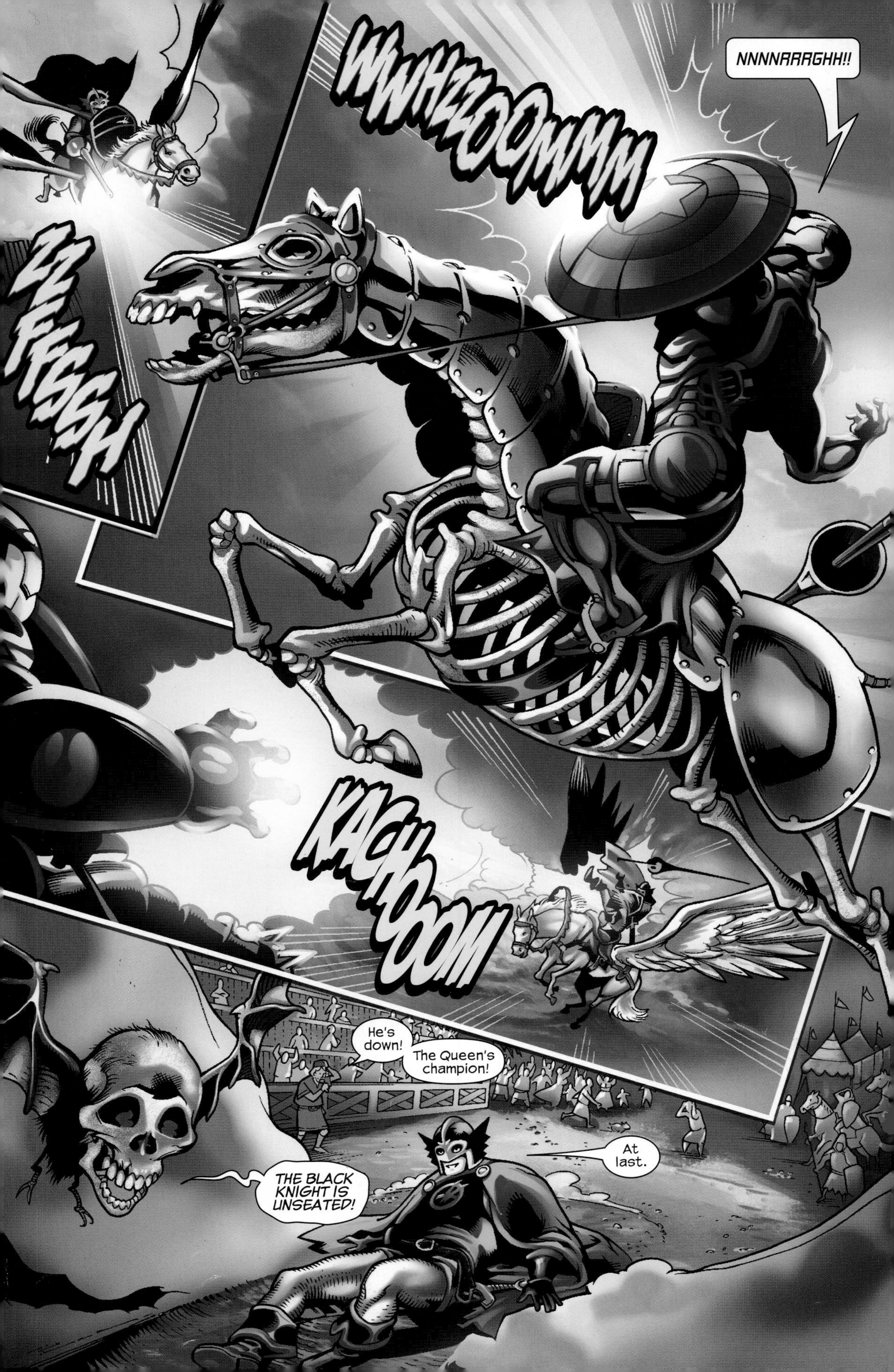
NNNNRRRGHH!!
WWHHZZOOMMMM
ZZFFSSSH
KACHOOOOM
He's down!
The Queen's champion!
THE BLACK KNIGHT IS UNSEATED!
At last.

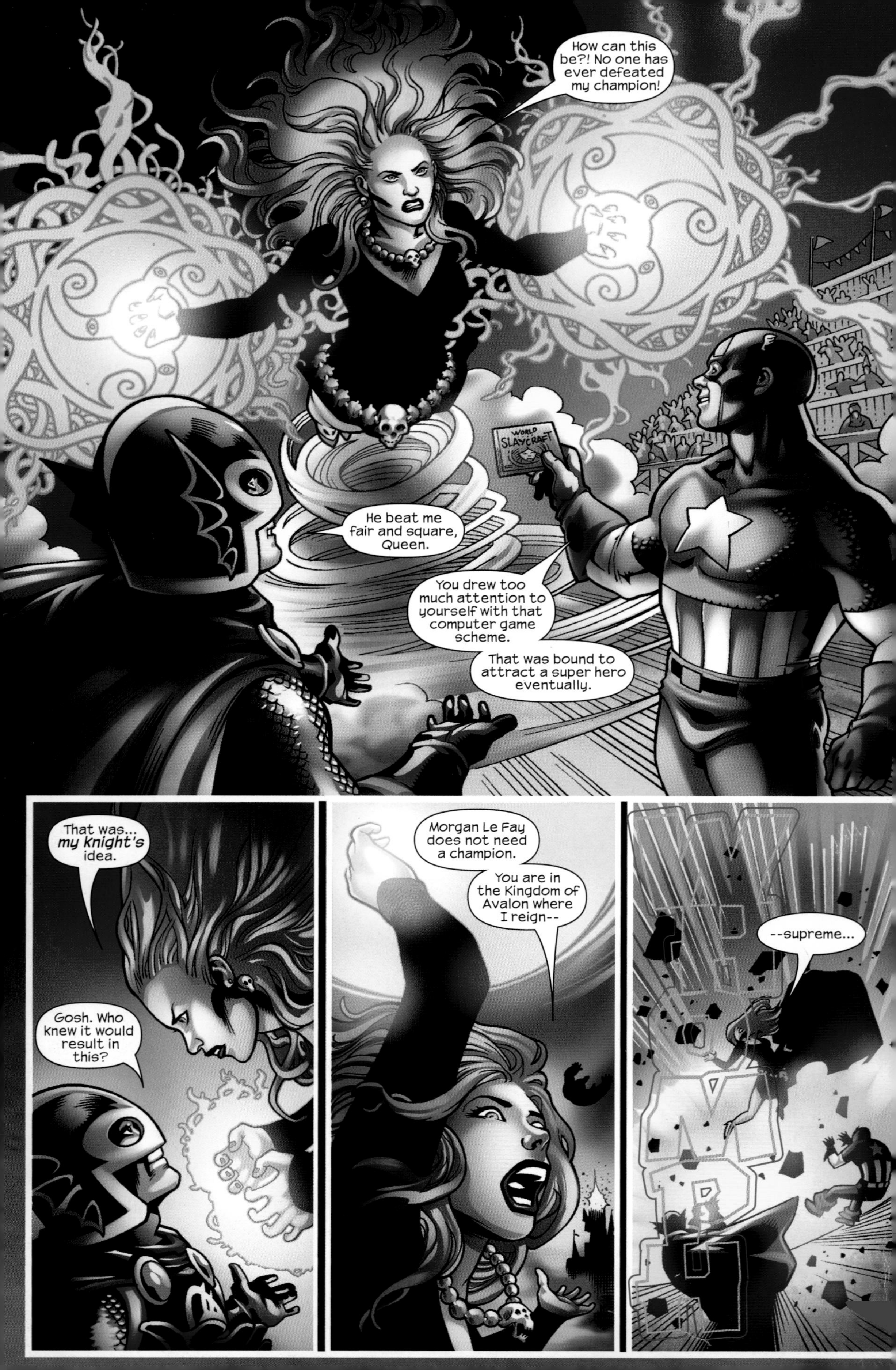
How can this be?! No one has ever defeated my champion!
He beat me fair and square, Queen.
You drew too much attention to yourself with that computer game scheme.
That was bound to attract a super hero eventually.
That was... *my knight's* idea.
Gosh. Who knew it would result in this?
Morgan Le Fay does not need a champion.
You are in the Kingdom of Avalon where I reign--
--supreme...

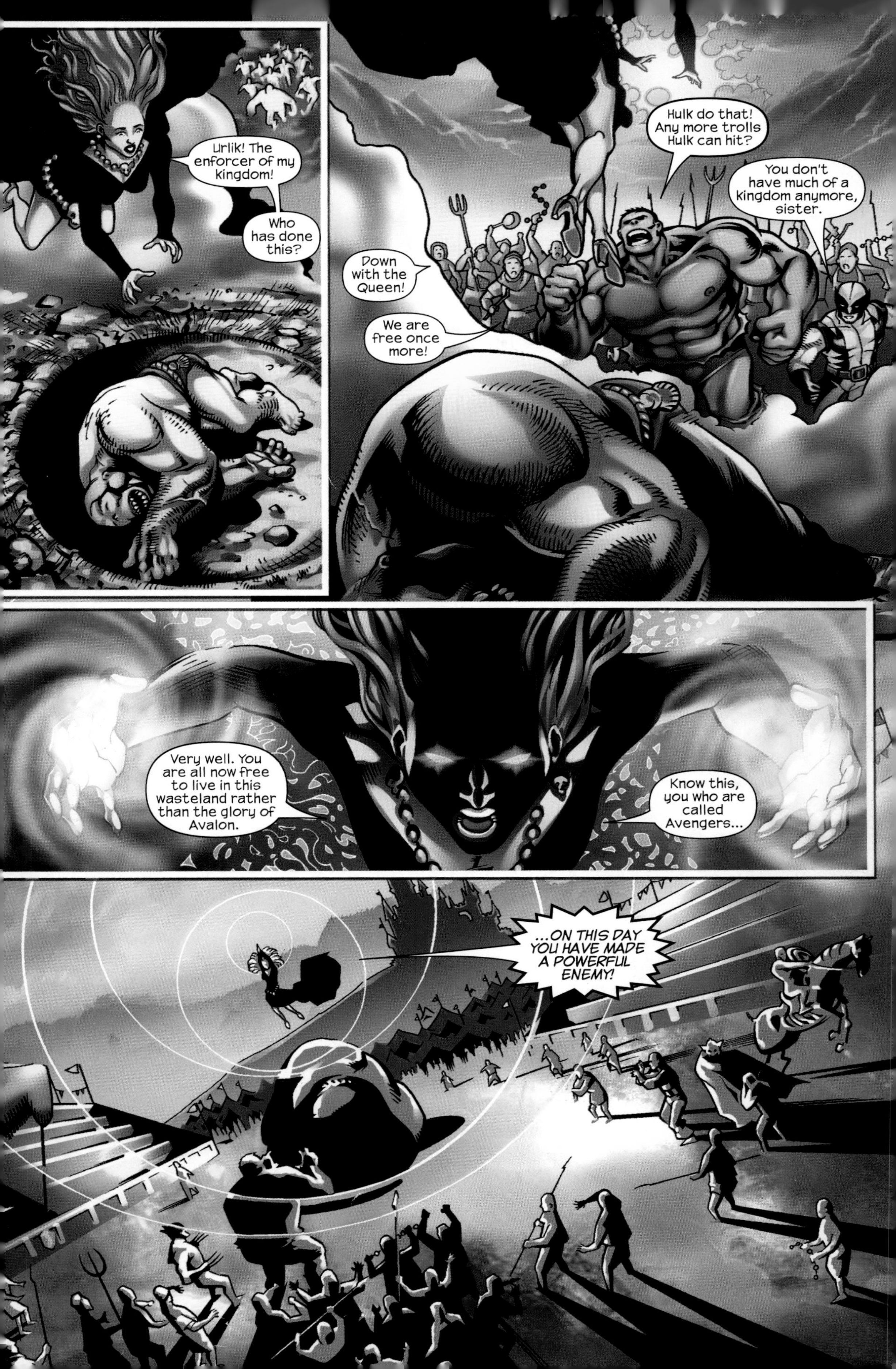
Urlik! The enforcer of my kingdom!
Who has done this?
Hulk do that! Any more trolls Hulk can hit?
You don't have much of a kingdom anymore, sister.
Down with the Queen!
We are free once more!
Very well. You are all now free to live in this wasteland rather than the glory of Avalon.
Know this, you who are called Avengers...
...ON THIS DAY YOU HAVE MADE A POWERFUL ENEMY!

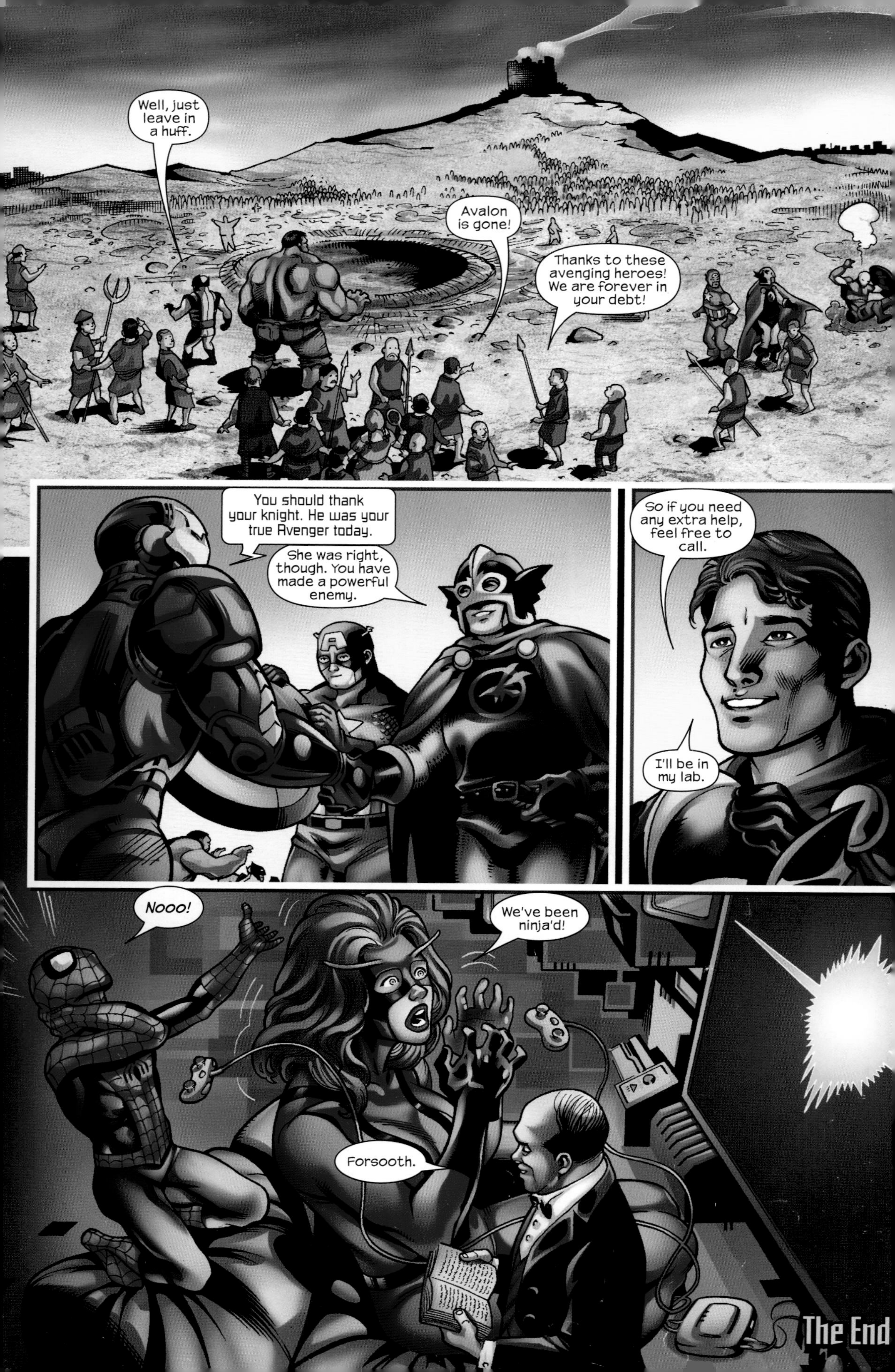
Well, just leave in a huff.
Avalon is gone!
Thanks to these avenging heroes! We are forever in your debt!
You should thank your knight. He was your true Avenger today.
She was right, though. You have made a powerful enemy.
So if you need any extra help, feel free to call.
I'll be in my lab.
Nooo!
We've been ninja'd!
Forsooth.
The End